Rebecca Price

Toby and the Flood

Floris Books

This edition published in 2008 by Floris Books

© 2008 Rebecca Price

Rebecca Price has asserted her right under the Copyright, Designs and Patents Act 1988
to be identified as the Author and Illustrator of this Work.

British Library CIP Data available

ISBN 978-086315-635-9

Printed in Singapore

Toby's bed was always wet when he woke up.

Mum tried using a sticker chart ...

She tried taking Toby to the toilet during the night ...

She even tried chocolate rewards ...

But nothing worked. Every morning Toby's bed was still wet.

Mum had to do lots of washing. Toby could see that she was annoyed, even though she tried not to show it.

"Don't worry," she sighed. "You'll get there in the end."

Toby hugged Mr Beaver, his favourite toy, and said nothing.

The next night Toby woke up. It was still dark but his bed was already soaked.

He tried to change his pyjamas as quietly as possible but his mum heard him and came to see what was happening.

Without saying a word, she pulled all the sheets off the bed, put new ones on, and went downstairs to the washing machine.

Toby climbed back into bed, but it was hard to get comfy.

Something was wrong ...

Mr Beaver was missing!

He looked everywhere but his toy had vanished.
Then Toby had a terrible thought: Mum must
have got Mr Beaver tangled up in the wet sheets.

He crept downstairs to the kitchen. The washing machine was whooshing around in the dark. He peered through the glass door. At first he couldn't see anything, but then a worried little face appeared for a moment before being swept away.

Poor Mr Beaver!

There was nothing Toby could do except wait until the washing machine finished. He settled into a laundry basket and watched the sheets going round and round.

After a while he began to feel as if he were spinning
with the washing.

He seemed to be flying between the sheets, high in the sky. Mr Beaver swooped by and Toby reached out to grab his furry paw.

Clutching Mr Beaver
tightly, Toby caught hold of
his duvet cover and used
it as a parachute to float
towards the ground.

Below him, a huge lake appeared and as he got closer he could see trees and houses sticking out of the water. He landed with a big splash, and waded across to a little girl who was gazing at the landscape.

"What's happened here?" asked Toby.
"Our valley has flooded," the girl replied. "If the water gets any higher, the animals will be in terrible danger."
"Perhaps we can help," said Toby. "Let's try and find out where the water is coming from."

Together, they splashed through the
flood until they arrived at the bottom
of a mountain.
An enormous waterfall was pouring
down the mountainside.
"I'm sure that wasn't there before,"
said the girl.

"Let's climb to the top of the waterfall," suggested Toby.
It was very steep but they helped each other up until finally, they reached a beautiful lake, surrounded by a high stone wall.

"Look!" shouted Toby. "The dam has broken over there. That's what's causing the flood. We need to fill the hole."

He tried to roll some stones into the water but they were too heavy. How were they ever going to mend the dam?

Crack!! Suddenly, there was a loud splitting noise and a tree crashed across the broken dam. Mr Beaver had used his sharp teeth to chop down the tree.

He cut down a few more trees, and showed Toby and the little girl how to fill up the gaps with small branches and mud. Soon the new dam was finished and the water stopped flowing out of the lake.

Laughing, Toby and his new friend started to slide back
down the mountain.
What a surprise! Instead of a vast lake, there were now
fields and meadows, houses and barns. The animals were
grazing happily, and all that was left of the flood was a
small pond.
But suddenly Toby realized that he needed a wee.
"How am I ever going to get home in time?" he panicked.

The little girl laughed.
"Don't you know that this is all a dream?"
she asked. "All you have to do is wake up!"
So, hoping she was right, Toby took a great
leap into the air ...

and jumped through the dream back to his house.

Dropping Mr Beaver, Toby rushed to the toilet ...

... just in time!

It was still dark outside.
Toby snuggled down with
Mr Beaver tucked safely in
his arms, and fell fast asleep
in his warm, DRY bed.